WITHDRAWN

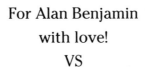

For Alan Benjamin
with love!
VS

For Kevin Donoghue
JB

This book is a presentation of Newfield Publications, Inc.
Newfield Publications offers book clubs for children
from preschool through high school. For further
information write to: **Newfield Publications, Inc.**
4343 Equity Drive, Columbus, Ohio 43228.

Published by arrangement with Lothrop, Lee & Shepard Books,
a division of William Morrow & Company, Inc.
Newfield Publications is a federally registered trademark of Newfield
Publications, Inc. Weekly Reader is a federally registered trademark
of Weekly Reader Corporation.

Library of Congress Cataloging-in-Publication Data. Selkowe, Valrie.
Spring green. Summary: Danny Duck needs something to take to a
"green" contest at a spring party and surprises himself by what he
actually takes. 1. Children's stories, American. [1. Green—Fiction.
2. Animals—Fiction. 3. Parties—Fiction] I. Bassett, Jeni, ill. II. Title.
PZ7.S456955Sp 1985   [E]   84-11202
   ISBN 0-688-04055-1   ISBN 0-688-04056-X (lib. bdg.)

Weekly Reader Children's Book Club Presents

Spring Green

Story by VALRIE M. SELKOWE
Pictures by JENI CRISLER BASSETT

Lothrop, Lee & Shepard Books • New York

 "Oh dear, oh dear, oh dear."

Danny waddled

back   and forth

   and all around.

"Are you looking for something you've lost?" T.J. asked him.

"No, I'm looking for something I can't find."

"Hi, T.J. Hi, Danny. What's up?"

"Oh hi, Chip.
I can't think of anything for the green contest at
Woody's spring party. The invitation
says whoever brings the most original
green thing is the winner."

"Why don't you take a leaf?"

"No! That's too common.
  I want something very special."

"Maybe a leaf is so common, no one else will bring one.
  I think I'll take it," said T.J.

"I'm taking this green apple,"
 said Chip.
"Isn't it a beauty?"

"Good enough to eat,"
 said T.J. "I hope you can hold off
 until after the contest."

"I need more time to think,"
  said Danny.

"Then we'll see you at the party," said Chip.

"Bye, Danny," said T.J.
"Don't be late."

"Maybe if I walk slowly
to Woody's house, I'll think
of something on the way."

"Oh dear, oh dear, oh dear."

"Hi, Danny! I'm taking a banana to Woody's party.
Do you think I'll win?"

"Bananas are yellow, Patch."

"Not if they aren't ripe yet! See you later!"

"Thatcher, what are you taking to the contest?"

"Lettuce," Thatcher answered, and hopped on his way.

"Everyone has something green
but me."

"Now there's something special!"

"Oh, it's you, Samantha.
I guess you're on your way to the party."

"What are you taking to the contest, Danny?"

"It's a secret," Danny answered.
"Even to me," he added
when she couldn't hear.

"There's Minton with a bright green ribbon."

"And Hooper has a big green crayon."

"Wait up, Danny!"

"Hi, Ricket, what did you bring for the contest?"

"Nothing," said Ricket. "I couldn't think of anything."

"Me neither," said Danny.

"It's too late now," said Ricket.

"Let's go in."

"Oh dear, oh dear, oh dear," said Danny.

"Hey, everybody! . . . Look!" shouted Woody.

"Yea!" everyone shouted at once.

"Danny is the winner!
Ricket the frog is the prize-winning green!"

Danny and Ricket beamed at each other.
Nobody knew their secret,
and they weren't about to tell.